To my little cousins, Linkoln, Aryll, Alyxis, and Davin.
Take my advice and stop getting older. You'll regret it later.

Text copyright © 2021 Springer Badger
First published in 2021 by Page Street Kids
an imprint of
Page Street Publishing Co.
27 Congress Street, Suite 105
Salem, MA 01970
www.pagestreetpublishing.com

Distributed by Macmillan, sales in Canada by The Canadian Manda Group

21 22 23 24 25 CCO 5 4 3 2 1
ISBN-13: 978-1-64567-287-6. ISBN-10: 1-64567-287-5

CIP data for this book is available from the Library of Congress.

This book was typeset in Chelsea Market Pro.
The illustrations were done with watercolor and digitally collaged.
Cover and book design by Melia Parsloe for Page Street Kids.
Printed and bound in Shenzhen, Guangdong, China.

Page Street Publishing uses only materials from suppliers who are committed to responsible and sustainable forest management.

Page Street Publishing protects our planet by donating to nonprofits like The Trustees, which focuses on local land conservation.

MOLES PRESENT

THE NATURAL TOLLS OF DIGGING HOLES

SPRINGER BADGER

PAGE STREET KIDS

Like moles in holes,
we dig in the ground.

We dig our holes deep
and we dig them round.

We dig holes for fun,
alone or in groups,

and holes for pipes
to get rid of poops.

But some holes get filled
with things that stink,

sometimes too close
to where we drink.

Some holes keep us safe
from what we dread.

We dig for treasure,
uncovering gold,

or finding remains
of things just as old.

We dig holes too deep
beneath the ocean

that sometimes leak
and cause a commotion.

Small holes for poles
where fish meet their ends,

and holes for warm fires
and feasting with friends.

But coal mines
and fracking lines

are holes dug from
damaging designs.

Holes for boats
and castle moats,

farming trenches,   dugout benches,

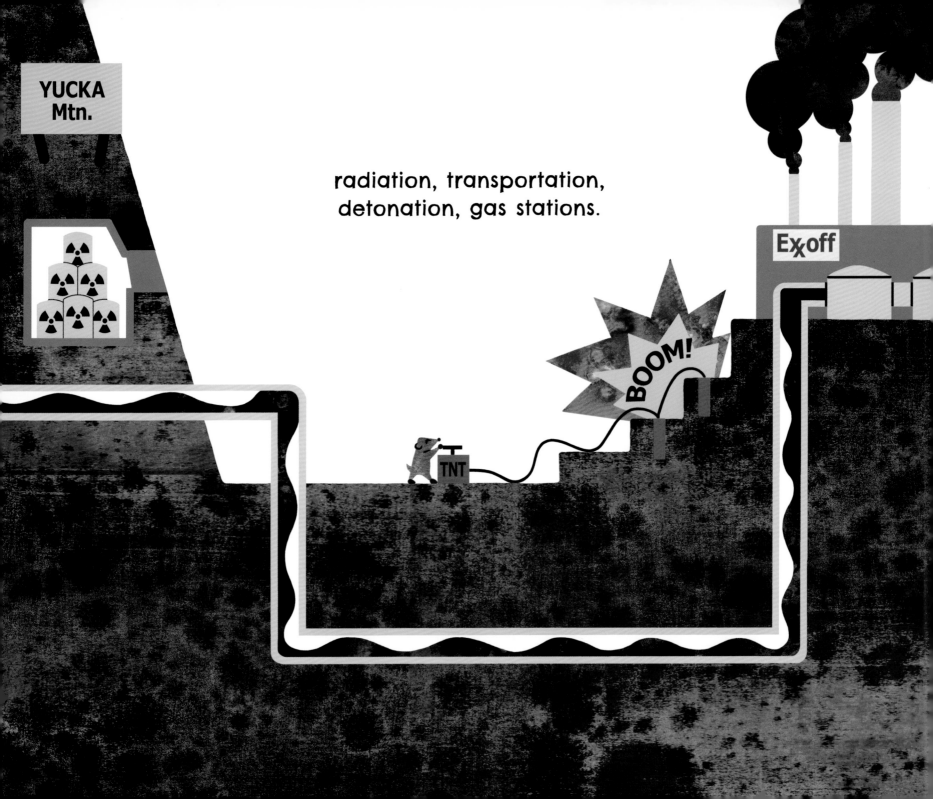

radiation, transportation, detonation, gas stations.

So many holes it's almost rude.
We even put holes in our food!

Ex off $8.99

Duncan's
Donuts

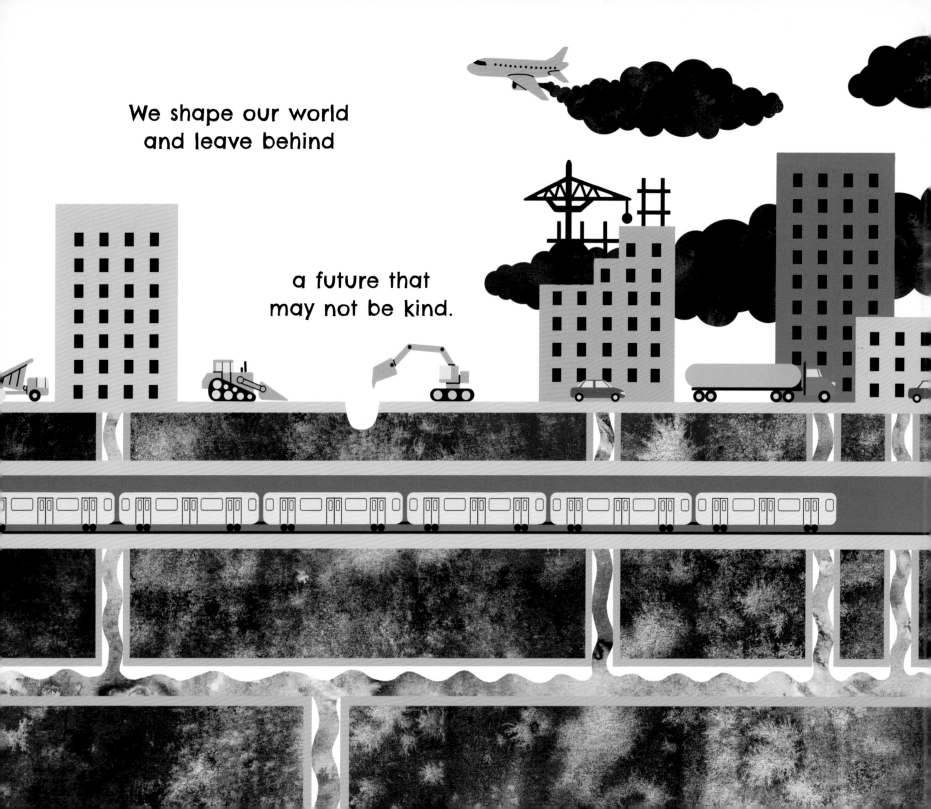

We shape our world
and leave behind

a future that
may not be kind.

So with the help of all the moles,
let's make something more than holes.